T0129644

THE
GRIFTAMOUSE
AND THE
STARDRAGON

A SLAMTO CARRACAS STORY

KATHLEEN KELLAIGH

BALBOA.
PRESS

A DIVISION OF HAY HOUSE

Copyright © 2019 Kathleen Kellaigh.

All rights reserved. No part of this book may be used or reproduced by any means, graphic, electronic, or mechanical, including photocopying, recording, taping or by any information storage retrieval system without the written permission of the author except in the case of brief quotations embodied in critical articles and reviews.

Balboa Press books may be ordered through booksellers or by contacting:

Balboa Press
A Division of Hay House
1663 Liberty Drive
Bloomington, IN 47403
www.balboapress.com
1 (877) 407-4847

Because of the dynamic nature of the Internet, any web addresses or links contained in this book may have changed since publication and may no longer be valid. The views expressed in this work are solely those of the author and do not necessarily reflect the views of the publisher, and the publisher hereby disclaims any responsibility for them.

The author of this book does not dispense medical advice or prescribe the use of any technique as a form of treatment for physical, emotional, or medical problems without the advice of a physician, either directly or indirectly. The intent of the author is only to offer information of a general nature to help you in your quest for emotional and spiritual well-being. In the event you use any of the information in this book for yourself, which is your constitutional right, the author and the publisher assume no responsibility for your actions.

Any people depicted in stock imagery provided by Getty Images are models, and such images are being used for illustrative purposes only.
Certain stock imagery © Getty Images.

ISBN: 978-1-9822-2439-4 (sc)
ISBN: 978-1-9822-2445-5 (e)

Print information available on the last page.

Balboa Press rev. date: 05/08/2019

Welcome to Apredasi! It is an island born in imagination and YOU help bring it to life!

The Slamto Carracas Stories have been read in grade schools and in adult performance forums with the same result: the audience is moved to draw what they are seeing, the fantastical creatures, the epic battles, the peaceful landscapes. (Even the cover art by Gregory Gwyn, came out of one of the readings!)

This book has been published with that in mind! Each person's imagination sees something different, and it seemed almost unfair to lock that in to one illustrator's art. So now you are on the creative team! Get out your crayons, markers, pencils, paint and brushes! You get to bring your visions of Slamto's friends to the page.

One of the great joys of sharing these stories has been receiving artwork afterwards! Please share with me on Instagram @kathleenkellaigh or on my Facebook page, Kathleen Kellaigh, Writer/Director (https://www.facebook.com/kkellaighwriter). Yo dossy!*

BONUS GAME:

 The letters of APREDASI can be re-arranged into another word! The new word also describes Apredasi!

APREDASI = ____ ____ ____ ____ ____ ____ ____ ____

*The meaning of "yo dossy" may be found in the glossary at the end of the book! The answer to the Apredasi anagram immediately follows... So solve the puzzle first!

PROLOGUE

SLAMTO CARRACAS

AND THE

SMIGLEYBUF BEAR

(This is the story of these two best friends!)

Slamto Carracas had a good life.
He lived on an island in the sea.
He ate cheff and honeymust each morning
And played with a clamto-eck-spurfi.

His yard was full of lanidostri,
Which, as you know, has quite a smell,
But it didn't bother Slamto Carracas
And he cared for them all very well.

He built a house with meck and rampus
And painted it a rare shade of gold,
And all who passed would stop to see it
And listen to the strange tales he told.

Yes, Slamto Carracas had a good life
For folks would come from near and far---
But one thing in his life was lacking,
So he wished on the Bossidodo Star:

"Oh, Bossidodo Star," said Slamto,
"My life is pretty fine, as you can see,
But what I really need to be happy,
Is a friend who will stay right here with me."

The Bossidodo Star blinked crimson
And silently shed a tear
That fell to the earth streaking silver,
And landed not too far from here.

But Slamto Carracas didn't notice,
For a miriwando boof flew by,
And called to the lonely little Slamto
As it circled him in the sky.

"Slamto," it sang in Drublick,
"Eclasto rampidy let fulblo."
And Slamto Carracas got the meaning,
Though his Drublick was just so-so.

A miriwando boof sings only
When a wish that is worthy to be,
Is about to come true any moment,
And Slamto felt his heart leap with glee.

"Yo dossy!" he yelled to the singer
Extending his arms to the sky.
The miriwando boof sang "'Welcome!"
And flitted to a tree nearby.

And then the miracle happened,
For right from the Bossidodo tear,
A glittering glow was forming
A perfect little Smigleybuf bear!

Now, Smigleys, I must tell you,
Have always been well-known
For their loyalty and devotion
Even when they are full-grown.

"Oh, just what I've always wanted!"
Cried Slamto joyfully,
"My very own Smigleybuf bear cub
To raise in my Quasidillo tree!"

Well, the Smigleybuf bear grew quickly,
As Smigleybuf bears often will
If they're fed blue leaves of Quasidillo
Until they have had their fill.

And Slamto Carracas loved the Smigley
And the Smigleybuf bear became
The most devoted friend in any nation
To bear the Smigleybuf name.

In the morning they ate together
And then they played till two
When Slamto told his stories
Till the scarlet sun withdrew.

Then all his guests would leave them
And the Smigleybuf bear would say,
"Woof de mao, my gentle Slamto,"
And they'd both walk down to the bay.

There they watched the waves together
Till the dancing stars appeared,
Then Slamto Carracas and the Smigley
Clapped their hands, and laughed and cheered.

And high in the sky above them,
The Bossidodo star blinked bright
And blessed the Smigleybuf and Slamto
With its most heart-warming light.

They said good night to each other
When the moon rose over the sea:
"Woof de mao, Smigleybuf," said Slamto.
"Woof de mao," said the loving Smigley.

And so they spent their lives together
In a friendship so very rare,
And when Slamto Carracas went to heaven
He still played with the Smigleybuf bear.

SMIGLEY'S FAVORITE TALE!

THE
GRIFTAMOUSE
AND THE
STARDRAGON

A Slamto Carracas Story

Slamto Carracas told this story
As folks from many countries gathered round,
And he placed his hand on the Smigley
Who sat next to him on the ground.

"My guests," said Slamto to the people
As they all sat just outside his house,
"Today I will tell of the Stardragon,
And the courage of a tiny Griftamouse.

"Many years ago, dear people,
Before any of us came to be
There was an extraordinary battle
In our very own galaxy."

(The Smigleybuf bear listened closely,
For you know, Smigley came from a star
And tales that were set in the heavens,
Were Smigley's special favorites, by far.)

"Perhaps you do not realize,"
Continued Slamto quietly,
"That every star above us
Has a life like you and me.

Well, there was a time before history,
When the stars were not very old,
That they felt they had to compete for space.
In fact, some became surprisingly bold.

And one had the heart of a dragon,
And one had the heart of a bear--
Not like my Smigleybuf, mind you,
But a beast quite ferocious and rare.

And they fought till the night sky turned scarlet,
While other stars looked fearfully on:
They would surely destroy one another!
The whole galaxy would be gone!

But far away from the battle
A star filled with wisdom blinked bright:
It's the star we now call Bossidodo
That we see almost every night.

The Bossidodo mustered all its power
And threw a beam like a lightning bolt
Giving the Starbear and Stardragon
A tremendously startling jolt.

And they heard deep in their star hearts
A rumbling like thousands of cries:
"Till you learn what it means to have friendship,
You are banished from the glittering skies."

And the Starbear disappeared from the heavens,
Falling to I don't know where,
But the Stardragon was hurled to this planet--
To this island that you and I share!

He terrorized all the people
Who were living in those days
And this awful Stardragon breathed fire
To set all of the mountains ablaze!

It seemed there was no one to save them--
Even the brave were afraid to go near
The hideous, enormous Stardragon
Who could wound simply with a sneer.

But one night, a tiny Griftamouse
Crept out and sniffed the air
And started the long journey
To the Stardragon's hidden lair.

People thought that a Griftamouse, you see,
Was the most useless creature alive,
And the Griftamouse knew that he wouldn't be missed,
Should the Stardragon not let him survive.

He reached the Mariftamo Mountains,
Where the Stardragon was thought to be,
And started to climb to the summit
Of the hill that was nearest the sea.

Suddenly the earth moved beneath him,
And the poor Griftamouse was aware
That the hill was in truth the Stardragon
Who had been sleeping outside his lair.

The Griftamouse stopped for a moment,
Then realized that he was too small
For the dragon to take any notice,
And so he continued to crawl.

He found himself next to an ear
Larger than a Remmybob tree,
And the Griftamouse paused to listen
To his heart beating frightfully.

Then it seemed like a quiet voice
Was telling him what to say,
And the Griftamouse spoke in a whisper
As the sun rose to start the day.

"Oh, Stardragon," said the Griftamouse,
"Why did you come to this land?
Why do you hurt all the people?
Please, I want to understand."

The Stardragon was surprised, naturally,
To hear a voice but see no one nearby.
And it surprised him even more, my friends,
To find himself anxious to reply.

He poured out to the Griftamouse
The sorrow of coming here
And how he longed to return to,
What he called "the heavenly sphere."

The Griftamouse listened closely,
And they passed the months of spring
Just getting to know one another.
How they'd talk, and laugh, and sing!

And never in those many days
Did the Stardragon ever see
The tiny Grift with the loving heart,
Who was his friend most certainly.

And one night in early summer
As they watched the pink moon rise,
The Bossidodo Star called the Stardragon
To return to his place in the skies.

Now the Griftamouse knew the Stardragon
Would be much happier in the sky,
But he had never had a real friend before
And the Griftamouse started to cry.

And as the Stardragon flew upward
He could finally see the Grift,
And the tears that he shed for this friendship,
Formed all the lakes of Marift.

The Griftamouse returned to his dwelling--
Indeed, he had not been missed--
The people of the land were still asking
"Why does the Grift exist?"

The Grift didn't bother to tell them
It was he who had saved the land.
He knew that they wouldn't believe him,
That they never would think him grand.

But every night, just after sunset,
The Griftamouse watched the stars rise,
And the Stardragon looking down from the heavens,
Saw the love in the little Grift's eyes.

"So you see, gentlefolk," said Slamto,
As the Smigley crawled onto his lap,
"Friendship is never something defined
By the borders on a map.

And it doesn't matter how tiny
Or how large the people are--
And no color can limit friendship,
And no distance is really too far.

For true friends are made in our hearts
And our hearts have no limits to love,
As the Griftamouse tells on this island,
And the Stardragon shows us from above.

And now my Smigleybuf Bear and I
Must leave you all, my dears,
For we have a date with a Griftamouse
To watch as his star appears."

SLAMTO CARRACAS' GUIDE TO THE WORDS OF APREDASI

APREDASI (a-preh-**dah'**-zee): an island where Slamto Carracas lives.

BOSSIDODO (**bahs'**-see-**doh'**-doh): a very specific, very powerful, very intelligent star that can be seen in the night sky.

CHEFF (chehf): a cereal-type food made from the grain of the rare cheffanut plant. The cheffanut grows only on the northern hills of the island of Apredasi.

CHEKAWEK (**chehk'**-a-wehk): a small, lovable creature thought to have mystical powers, found only in the mountains of Rampledeck.

CLAMTO-ECK-SPURFI (**clam'**-toh-ehk-**spur'**-fee): a rather dull, large but harmless creature at home both in the sea and on land.

GRIFTAMOUSE (**grif'**-ta-mous): a tiny, undistinguished creature who lives very much alone and is not generally liked by people.

HONEYMUST (**huh'**-nee-must): a sweet milk-like liquid produced by the Krinklebee Cow, a small gentle creature who dines on lanidostri.

LANIDOSTRI (la-ni-**dahs'**-tree): a flowering plant native to the island of Apredasi that has a strong though not unpleasant scent. It is the main diet of the Krinklebee Cow.

MARIFTAMO (mah-**rif'**-tah-moh): a region of lakes and mountains along the eastern coast of the island of Apredasi.

MECK (mehk): a building material used on the island of Apredasi made with shells.

MIRAWANDO BOOF (mi-rah-**wahn'**-doh boof'): an extremely rare flying creature, with brightly colored feathers, and an enchanting singing voice. The mirawando boof sings in the ancient language of Drublick.

MISTIREGA (mis-ti-**ray'**-gah): the name of a magical wind.

71

RAMPUS (**ram'**-puhs): a fiber made from the rample vines that grow on the island of Apredasi. (These vines orignally were found in Rampledeck and transported to Apredasi by visiting merchants).

REMMYBOB (**rem'**-mee-bahb): a tree that is large and wide with spreading branches and huge leaves.

WOOF DE MAO (**whoof'** deh **maow'**): These words translate best to "I love you".

YO DOSSY (yoh **dahs'**-see): "Thank you" in Drublick.

Bonus Game Answer:

APREDASI is an anagram for PARADISE

Printed in the United States
By Bookmasters

Printed in the United States
By Bookmasters